Dear Parents,

Welcome to the Scholastic Reader series. We have taken over 80 years of experience with teachers, parents, and children and put it into a program that is designed to match your child's interests and skills.

Level 1—Short sentences and stories made up of words kids can sound out using their phonics skills and words that are important to remember.

Level 2—Longer sentences and stories with words kids need to know and new "big" words that they will want to know.

Level 3—From sentences to paragraphs to longer stories, these books have large "chunks" of texts and are made up of a rich vocabulary.

Level 4—First chapter books with more words and fewer pictures.

It is important that children learn to read well enough to succeed in school and beyond. Here are ideas for reading this book with your child:

- Look at the book together. Encourage your child to read the title and make a prediction about the story.
- Read the book together. Encourage your child to sound out words when appropriate. When your child struggles, you can help by providing the word.
- Encourage your child to retell the story. This is a great way to check for comprehension.
- Have your child take the fluency test on the last page to check progress.

Scholastic Readers are designed to support your child's efforts to learn how to read at every age and every stage. Enjoy helping your child learn to read and love to read.

　　　　—Francie Alexander
　　　　　Chief Education Officer
　　　　　Scholastic Education

To Ginger — The original Invisible-Visible Dog
— E.L.

In Memory of the Amazing June Grammer
— D.B.

Text copyright © 1995 by Elizabeth Levy.
Illustrations copyright © 1995 by Denise Brunkus.
Activities copyright © 2003 Scholastic Inc.

Library of Congress Cataloging-in-Publication Data is available.

ISBN 0-590-47484-7

10 9 8 7

07

Printed in the U.S.A.   23
First printing, August 1995

INVISIBLE INC.

The Mystery of the Missing Dog

by Elizabeth Levy

Illustrated by Denise Brunkus

Scholastic Reader — Level 4

Cartwheel
·B·O·O·K·S·®

SCHOLASTIC INC.
New York   Toronto   London   Auckland   Sydney
Mexico City   New Delhi   Hong Kong   Buenos Aires

Meet Invisible Inc.

Except for his tail, Chip's dog, Max, was invisible! So was Chip. But at least Chip wore clothes.

Last summer, Chip and Max were in a cave. They fell into a pool of water. When they came out, they were both invisible. Chip's clothes were invisible, too.

Soon Chip's family, his friends, and almost everyone in Chip's town got used to Chip. But no one except

his good friends, Charlene and
Justin, knew about his invisible
clothes. With them, Chip could go
totally invisible. Chip kept them in
his backpack.

Justin had a hearing loss, and he
could read lips. He looked at things
very carefully. He often noticed
things that others didn't. Charlene
was very good at figuring things out.
Together, the three of them started
Invisible Inc. to solve mysteries.
They right wrongs others don't see.

And just for fun, the kids write
their notes with invisible ink!

CHAPTER 1
Where's That Max?

"Here, Max!" shouted Chip. Chip and his friends were going to take Chip's dog to the dog show. But where was he?

Suddenly, the TV went on by itself. And it was LOUD! Programs flashed across the screen.

"Max has the remote again!" said Chip.

"There it is!" shouted Justin.

The remote was floating in the air.

Justin jumped at the remote, but he could not get it. The remote flew across the room — followed by a little brown dot.

Charlene held out her hands.

"I've got him!" she shouted.

She handed the remote to Chip.

"Bad dog," she said to Max.

"He may not know how to use the remote control, but he does have a new trick for the dog show," said Chip.

Chip put a mitten in a hat, then clapped his hands. The mitten flew out of the hat and across the room. It was followed by the brown wagging dot.

"That's neat!" said Charlene. "The judges will love it."

"But the judges won't be able to see him," said Justin.

Chip was sad. "You're right. The judges won't give a prize to a dog they can't see."

"We can dye Max," said Charlene. "We can use food coloring."

Charlene mixed the food coloring, and Chip put Max in the tub. Brown water flew everywhere.

Now Max was visible. He was a deep chocolate brown.

"I hope he doesn't lick this stuff off," said Justin.

At the park was a huge sign: K-9 FUN FEST.

Max wagged his tail. He loved to be with other dogs.

Chip, Charlene, and Justin met Mary and Sandy, two girls from their class.

"Do you have a dog?" Justin asked.

Mary shook her head. "We just came to watch."

"My father is allergic to dogs," said Sandy.

Max's tail wagged. Chip held his leash tighter. A huge Doberman pinscher barked.

"Watch it!" said the boy who was holding the big dog's leash.

Chip pulled Max's leash. It wrapped around Mary's legs and she fell on the big dog.

"Be careful," said the boy. "You'll hurt my champion!"

Mary looked scared.

"Your dog could have hurt Mary," said Chip.

"My dog is a purebred," said the boy. "And I can see that yours is not."

"Chip's dog may not be a pure-bred, but he has a pure heart," said Charlene.

"My dog is a champion. She always wins," said the boy. "She can do anything that your dog can do — but better."

"Well, *this* dog can disappear," said Charlene. "Can your dog do that?"

While the children talked, the two dogs licked each other. And Max started to disappear!

The boy was very surprised. He walked away, dragging his dog behind him.

"What happened to that dog?" a woman shouted. She had bright-red hair and wore purple clothes.

"He's invisible," said Charlene.

"Amazing!" said the woman. A low
growl came from under her cape. A
tiny dog with big ears peeked out.

"Amazing!" the woman said again. Then she walked away.

"She's strange," said Justin.

"We'll have to dye Max again," said Chip.

"I'm hungry," Charlene said. "Let's have lunch first."

Charlene, Justin, and Chip walked to the food stand. On the way, they passed the snobby boy with his big dog, the strange woman with her little dog, and Sandy and Mary with no dog at all.

The children ordered nachos. A tortilla chip with gooey cheese on it dropped to the ground.

"It's okay, Max. You can eat it," said Chip.

But the nacho just lay on the ground.

"Why isn't Max eating the nacho?" Justin asked.

Chip tugged on Max's leash. It was slack.

"He's not here!" Chip shouted. "Someone took Max!"

CHAPTER 2
Lost — One Dog
You Can't See

Chip, Justin, and Charlene searched the park for Max. They called his name again and again. But no little brown tail came wagging.

They asked the snobby boy, the strange woman, Sandy, and Mary if they knew where Max could be. They all said no.

"This is a case for Invisible Inc.!" said Charlene.

"Right," groaned Chip. "We can put up posters: 'Lost — One Dog You Can't See!' I suppose you'll want to write the posters in invisible ink, too."

"Don't be silly," said Charlene. "Justin can make great posters."

Justin was a very good artist. He made posters that showed Max's brown tail. The large, red letters announced:

Chip, Charlene, and Justin put the signs up all over the park. Justin put one on a tree and noticed another poster nearby.

"Hey, look at this!" he said. "That lady was a magician." He pointed to a picture of the woman with the red hair. AMAZING GRACE read the poster. CALL TODAY! WE DO MAGIC SHOWS FOR BIRTHDAY PARTIES.

Charlene started to write something down on her pad.

"What are you doing?" Chip asked.

"Taking her address and phone number," said Charlene. "I might want a magician at my next birthday party."

By the end of the day, nobody had turned in an invisible dog with a dot of a tail.

On their way out of the park, Chip, Justin, and Charlene ran into the snobby boy from the dog show.

"Have you seen our dog, Max, anywhere?" asked Charlene. "He seemed to like your dog. Maybe he followed her."

"You keep your dog away from my Millie," warned the boy. "I don't like her licking all of that food coloring." He tugged on Millie's leash and left.

"I think he knows where Max is," said Chip. "I'm going to follow him."

Chip ran behind a tree. He put on his invisible clothes. Chip's invisibility could come in handy at times like this.

Fifteen minutes later, Chip returned, huffing.

"Well, I didn't find Max," said Chip. "But I did find out that boy's name. I heard his mother call for him from her car — William Watson the Third."

"But did you find any clues about Max?" asked Justin.

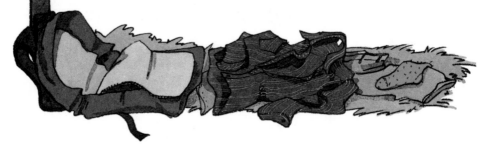

"Not exactly," said Chip. "But I don't trust that William Watson the Third. I know he has something to do with Max disappearing."

Charlene frowned. "A good detective doesn't jump to conclusions."

"She's right," said Justin. "Just because he wants his dog to win doesn't mean he did it."

"But if he didn't," asked Chip as he put his visible clothes back on, "who did?"

CHAPTER 3
Amazing Dog Tricks

On their way home, the members of Invisible Inc. saw Mary. She was carrying a shopping bag from the dog show.

"I saw your posters," said Mary. "Did you find Max yet?"

"No," said Charlene, looking sad. "We've looked everywhere for him."

"It would be amazing if you find him," said Mary. "There are so many dogs here, and you can't even see Max."

"What did you say?" Justin asked.

Mary turned to face him. She knew Justin could read her lips better if she looked straight at him.

"I said it would be amazing if you found him," repeated Mary.

"Amazing . . ." Justin said to himself.

Mary looked at him strangely. "I've got to go," she said, clutching her shopping bag. "I hope you find Max."

"I don't see what's so amazing," complained Charlene. "We haven't found Max, and we don't even have any clues."

"Who would want an invisible dog?" Justin asked slowly. "Use your head."

Chip scratched his head and thought.

Suddenly, Charlene's eyes lit up. "Amazing Grace!" she shouted.

"Right!" said Justin. "A magician would have a million uses for an invisible dog. I'll bet she has Max."

"But how can we find out for sure?" asked Charlene.

"Let's go to her house and pretend that we want to hire her for a birthday party," said Chip. He turned to Charlene. "You have her address, right?"

Charlene took out her pad. She had used her special Invisible Inc. pen, filled with lemon juice, to write the address.

"We need something warm so we can read it," said Justin. He ran back to the park and bought a hot chocolate at the refreshment stand.

Charlene held the paper over the steam from the cup. As soon as the address appeared, they were off.

Amazing Grace lived in a very strange house. It was painted pink and had shutters with blue stars.

Charlene rang the doorbell. Amazing Grace answered the door, carrying her Chihuahua and a shopping bag of dog food from the show.

"Yes?" said the woman.

"We're having a birthday party," said Chip, "and we saw your poster in the park. Can you do tricks with dogs in your magic show?"

Amazing Grace laughed as she invited them in.

"Can I do tricks with dogs? Watch this!" she said. "Merlin — fetch!"

The little dog jumped on Charlene's shoulder and pulled a quarter out from behind her ear.

"Wow!" said Charlene. "How did you teach him to do that?"

"A good magician never reveals her secrets," said Grace, smiling. "Now, when are you planning to have this party?"

Before Charlene could answer, Justin interrupted.

"May I have that?" he asked, pointing to the shopping bag on the floor.

The magician smiled at him. She took out several cans of dog food from the bag and turned it inside out.

"Whoops! It's not empty," said Grace. She pulled out a bunch of

paper flowers and handed them to
Justin.

"That was great!" said Chip.

"Thanks," said Justin, as he
returned the flowers, "but I just
want the bag. Thanks again!" he
shouted as he ran out of the house.
Chip and Charlene followed.

"What's gotten into you?" asked
Charlene. "Why did you want that
bag?"

"There's no time to explain," said
Justin. "I think I know who took
Max. We've been barking up the
wrong tree!"

CHAPTER 4
Canine Clues

"At last. A real clue!" Justin said, pointing to the shopping bag. The words *Debbie's Delicious Dog Food* were printed on the side. "We've seen this shopping bag before."

"We have?" said Charlene and Chip together.

Justin nodded. "This is the same shopping bag that Mary had. Mary doesn't have a dog. She has a salamander. Why would she buy dog food for a salamander?"

"Because she has Max!" exclaimed Charlene.

"Exactly!" declared Justin.

Charlene started down the street. "Come on. Let's go to Mary's house."

"Wait," said Justin. "We have to
have a plan."

"We don't have time for a plan,"
said Chip. "It's getting dark. I have
to find Max."

They ran to Mary's house and rang the bell. Mary came to the door.

"Hi, guys," she said. "Any luck finding Max?"

"No," said Justin, spotting the shopping bag on the floor. He picked it up and lifted out a can of dog food.

"Why did you buy dog food?" asked Justin.

"Uh — I — I — a friend asked me to buy it for her new dog," Mary stammered, turning red.

"We think you bought it for an invisible dog," Charlene blurted out.

Justin rolled his eyes. He knew that a good detective doesn't accuse a suspect until all of the evidence is in.

"Max isn't here," said Mary. "You can search the house if you want to."

Charlene and Justin headed for the den, but Chip sank down on a chair. He knew Max wasn't there. If Max were there, he would have come running.

"I may never see Max again," said Chip.

"We're sorry, Mary," said Justin. "We shouldn't have blamed you."

"I'm sure Max is all right," said Mary.

"I'm not," Chip said, standing up. "I guess I should go home." For a moment he looked hopeful. "Maybe Max is waiting there for me."

"Good idea," said Mary, trying to cheer him up.

Chip raced down the street, with Justin and Charlene following close behind. But when they got to Chip's house, there was no wagging tail. There was no Max at all.

CHAPTER 5
Lost and Found

The next day, Chip was almost too unhappy to go to the dog show. "But you have to go," said Charlene. "Max just might show up there."

When they got there, as always, Charlene was hungry. "Come on," she said. "Let's go get a hot dog."

"Who could eat a hot dog at a time like this?" asked Chip.

Justin sighed. "You go, Charlene. I'll stay with Chip. Bring me back a hot dog, too."

Charlene bought the hot dogs and stopped at a souvenir stand on the way back. William Watson the Third strutted by with Millie at his side. "Did your friend ever find his dog?" he asked.

Charlene shook her head.

"Too bad," William said. "I guess he's a *no show.*"

"That's mean," said Charlene. "You wouldn't like it if someone took Millie."

William Watson the Third looked a little embarrassed. He picked up a stuffed rabbit. When he squeezed it, it barked. "I bet Millie would love fetching this," said William.

"Hey, I'm buying that," said Mary's friend, Sandy. She grabbed the toy and paid for it.

"She sure is in a hurry," said William.

Charlene stared at Sandy's back. Taking out her fountain pen, she wrote on a napkin in invisible ink and gave it to William Watson the Third.

"Will you run and give this to
Chip and Justin?" she asked.

William looked at the napkin. "It's
blank."

"Please do it," Charlene begged.

"Why should I do you a favor?" William Watson the Third asked.

"Think how you would feel if someone took Millie," said Charlene.

"I'd hate it," said William Watson the Third. He took the paper.

"Take these to them, too," said Charlene as she gave him the hot dogs. "I've got to run. They'll know what to do." Charlene took off after Sandy.

William Watson the Third brought the napkin and hot dogs to Justin and Chip.

"What's this?" asked Justin, taking the napkin. "Another joke?"

"Your friend Charlene asked me to give it to you," said William. "She said you'd know what to do." He handed Chip the hot dogs. "I hope you find your dog."

"Thanks," said Chip. "Thanks a lot." William smiled a little and walked away, with Millie following close behind.

Justin held the napkin over the heat of the hot dog. The words

appeared.

"Let's go!" shouted Justin.

Chip was already ahead of him.

When they got to Sandy's house, Charlene was hiding behind a tree.

"Do you see Max?" Chip whispered urgently.

Charlene shook her head. "No. But listen."

"I don't hear anything," said Justin.

But Chip heard a bark. "It's Max!" he said excitedly. He ran to the front door before Justin could stop him.

Sandy's father answered the bell.

"Excuse me," said Chip, trying to be polite. "But I think you may have my dog."

"We don't allow dogs in our home," said Sandy's dad. He sneezed and rubbed at his red eyes. "I'm allergic to them."

Suddenly, a bark came from inside the house. Sandy came to the door carrying the stuffed rabbit she had bought at the show. "It's my new toy," she said. "It's a rabbit that barks."

Sandy's father sneezed again. "I seem to be allergic even to toy rabbits that bark like dogs."

Chip looked discouraged.
"Another false alarm."

Just as the door was closing,
Chip heard another bark.

Chip ran to Justin and Charlene.
"I know Max's bark. That *is* him in
there — somewhere. I've got to go
invisible. You and Charlene ring the
doorbell again."

"What am I going to say?" asked
Justin.

"Say anything," said Chip, quickly
changing into his invisible clothes.
"Just give me a chance to get
inside."

Charlene and Justin rang the
doorbell. "Hello. Can I help you with
something?" Sandy's mother asked
them.

"Uh . . . we're collecting money for
animal rescue," Charlene said
quickly. "We find lost animals."

Sandy's mother smiled. "How
nice. I'll get some change."

While they waited by the open door, Chip slipped inside. Moments later, a streak of a brown tail came flying out of the house.

"What was that?" asked Sandy's mother.

Sandy ran down the stairs and out of the house.

"Excuse us," said Charlene. She and Justin ran after Sandy.

Chip was waiting behind a tree. A little brown dot wagged back and forth in Chip's arms. "Good boy!" said Chip, hugging Max tightly. "Good dog!"

Sandy heard Max barking and saw the brown dot.

"I'm sorry," she said. "I just took him as an experiment. I thought maybe my dad wouldn't be allergic to an invisible dog.

"I asked Mary to buy some dog food for Max yesterday and then I was going to bring him back. But Mary told me how worried you all were. I was scared that you would be angry with me. But honestly, I would have brought him back to you tonight."

"By then he would have missed the whole dog show," said Charlene.

Chip looked down at the wagging brown dot. "He doesn't have a chance. The judges can't see him. And there's no time to use food coloring on him now."

"Wait a minute," said Charlene. "Max can pull a rabbit out of a hat."

"He can do what?" asked Chip.

Charlene explained her plan.

Chip giggled and looked at Sandy.

"We'll have to borrow your stuffed rabbit," he said.

"Of course," said Sandy. "It's the least I can do."

They ran back to the dog show. Chip walked into the ring with Max. To everyone else, it looked as if Chip was walking a pretend dog on a trick leash.

"What's this?" asked a judge.

"This is my dog, Max," said Chip.

The judge knelt down. His hand became wet as Max slobbered kisses on his knuckles.

"It *is* a dog," said the judge.

"And he's officially entered," said another judge, looking at her list.

"It's highly unusual," said one judge to the other.

They read their rule book.

"There is no rule against invisible dogs," said the first judge.

Max trotted smartly by Chip's side, heeling perfectly when Chip stopped. Justin, Charlene, Sandy, and Mary all cheered loudly. William Watson the Third even gave Chip a thumbs-up sign.

Chip put his baseball cap down in the center of the ring.

"Presenting the Amazing Max!" he cried.

He clapped his hands. Quick as a blink, a brown dot shot across the ring and hovered over the hat.

"Abracadabra!" shouted Chip.

The rabbit jumped out of the hat and floated through the air, landing at the feet of the judges.

Max and Chip won first prize in the Silly Dog Trick category. After the show, Chip carried his blue ribbon over to his friends.

"I guess you just can't keep an invisible dog down," he said proudly.

"Your dog is amazing," said a familiar voice.

Chip turned to see Amazing Grace and her Chihuahua. She handed Chip her business card.

"Perhaps we can do business together," she said.

Chip reached into his pocket and handed her an official Invisible Inc. card.

"It's blank," said Amazing Grace.

"It's not blank. It's invisible," said Charlene.

"Invisible Inc. at your service," added Justin.

Amazing Grace took the card and smiled. "Amazing," she whispered.

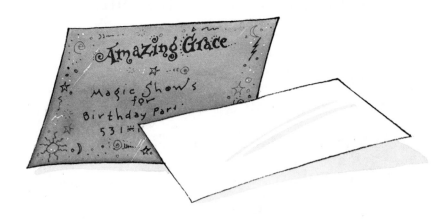